KU-394-500

Winnie-the-Pooh
A Very Grand Thing

Adapted from the stories by A.A. Milne

Halfway between Pooh's house and Piglet's house there was a Thoughtful Spot where they met sometimes when they had decided to go and see each other.

One autumn morning, when the wind had blown all the leaves off the trees in the night, and was trying to blow the branches off too, Pooh and Piglet were sitting in the Thoughtful Spot and wondering who to visit.

"Let's go and see *everybody*," said Pooh. "Because when you've been walking in the wind for miles and you suddenly go into somebody's house and he says, 'Hallo, Pooh, you're just in time for a little smackerel of something,' and you are, then that's what I call a Friendly Day."

Piglet thought they ought to have a Reason for going to see everybody, like Looking for Small or Organising an Expotition, if Pooh could think of something.

Pooh could think of something.

"We'll go because it's Thursday," he said. 'We'll wish everybody a Very

Happy Thursday. Come on, Piglet."

They got up and when Piglet had sat down again, because he didn't know the wind was so strong, and had been helped up again by Pooh, they started off.

They went to Pooh's house first, and luckily Pooh was at home just as they got there, so he asked them in, and they had some, and then they went on to Kanga's house. They were holding on to each other and shouting, "Isn't it?" and "What?" and "I can't hear."

By the time they got to Kanga's house, they were so buffeted by the wind that they stayed to lunch. When they left, at first it seemed rather cold outside, so they pushed on to Rabbit's as quickly as they could.

When they got there, Pooh said to Rabbit, "We've come to wish you a Very Happy Thursday." Then he went in and out of the door once or twice just to make sure that he *could* get out again.

"What's happening on Thursday?" asked Rabbit.
Pooh explained and Rabbit, whose life was made up of
Important Things, said, "Oh, I thought you'd really

come to see me about something."
Then they sat down for a little . . . and by-and-by, Pooh
and Piglet went on again. The wind was behind them
now, so they didn't have to shout to each other.

Christopher Robin was at home by this time, because it was the afternoon. He was so glad to see Pooh and Piglet that they stayed there until very nearly teatime. They had a Very Nearly Tea, which is one you forget about afterwards. Then they hurried on to Pooh Corner, to see Eeyore before it was too late to have a Proper Tea with Owl.

"Hallo, Eeyore," they called out cheerfully.

"Ah!" said Eeyore. "Have you lost your way?"

"We just came to see you," said Piglet. "And to see how your house was. Look, Pooh, it's still standing!"

"I know," said Eeyore. "Very odd. Somebody ought to have come down and pushed it over."

"We wondered whether the wind would blow it down," said Pooh.

"Ah, that's why nobody's bothered, I suppose. I thought perhaps they'd forgotten."

Pooh and Piglet shuffled about a little and said, "Well, goodbye, Eeyore," as lingeringly as they could. But they had a long way to go, and they wanted to be getting on to Owl's house.

The wind was against them now, and Piglet's ears streamed out behind him like banners as he fought his way along. It seemed like hours before he got them into

the shelter of the Hundred Acre Wood. There, they stood up straight again, to listen a little nervously to the roaring of the gale among the treetops.

"Supposing a tree fell down, Pooh, when we were underneath it?" said Piglet.

"Supposing it didn't," said Pooh after careful thought.

Piglet was comforted by this. In a little while, Pooh and Piglet were knocking cheerfully at Owl's door.

"Hallo, Owl," said Pooh. "I hope we're not too late for – I mean, how are you, Owl? Piglet and I just came to see how you were because it's Thursday."

"Sit down, Pooh. Sit down, Piglet," said Owl kindly. "Make yourselves comfortable."

They thanked him and then made themselves as comfortable as they could.

"Because, you see, Owl," said Pooh, "we've been hurrying, so as to be in time for – so as to see you before we went away again."

Owl nodded solemnly.

"Correct me if I am wrong," he said, "but am I right in supposing that it is a very blusterous day outside?"

"Very," said Piglet, who was quietly thawing his ears, and wishing that he was safely back in his own house.

"I thought so," said Owl. "It was on just such a blusterous day as this that my Uncle Robert, a portrait of whom you see hanging upon the wall on your right, Piglet, while returning in the late forenoon from a – what was that?"

There was a loud cracking noise.

"Look out!" cried Pooh. "Mind the clock! Out of
the way, Piglet! Piglet, I'm falling on you!"

"Help!" cried Piglet.

Pooh's side of the room was slowly tilting upwards and his chair began sliding down on Piglet's. The clock slithered gently along the mantelpiece, collecting vases on the way, until they all crashed together on to what had once been the floor, but was now a wall.

Uncle Robert, who was trying to be the new hearthrug, and was bringing the rest of his wall with him, met Piglet's chair just as Piglet was expecting to leave it. For a little while, it became very difficult to remember which was really the north. Then there was another loud crack . . .

Owl's room collected itself
feverishly . . . and there was silence.
Then, in a corner of the room, the
tablecloth began to wriggle.

Then it wrapped itself into a ball
and rolled across the room. Then it
jumped up and down once or twice
and put out two ears, revealing Piglet!

"Pooh," said Piglet, nervously.

"Yes?" said one of the chairs.

"Where are we?"

"I'm not quite sure," said the chair.

"Are we still in Owl's House?"

"I think so," said Pooh, "because we were just going to have tea, and we hadn't had it yet."

"Oh!" said Piglet, in surprise. "Did Owl *always* have a letterbox in his ceiling?"

"Has he?" said Pooh.

"Yes, look."

"I can't," said Pooh. "I'm face downwards under something, and that Piglet, is a very bad position for looking at ceilings."

"Well, he has, Pooh," said Piglet.

"Perhaps he's changed it round," said Pooh. "Just for a change."

There was a disturbance behind the table in the other corner of the room, and then Owl was back with them again.

"Ah, Piglet," said Owl, looking very much annoyed, "where's Pooh?"

"I'm not quite sure," said Pooh.

Owl turned at his voice, and frowned towards as much of Pooh as he could see.

"Pooh," said Owl severely, "did *you* do that?"

"No," said Pooh humbly. "I don't *think* so."

"Then who did?" said Owl.

"I think it was the wind," said Piglet. "I think your house has blown down!"

"Oh, is that it? I thought it was Pooh," said Owl.

"No," said Pooh.

"If it was the wind," said Owl, considering the matter, "then it wasn't Pooh's fault and no blame can be attached to him."

With these kind words, Owl and Piglet pushed and pulled at the armchair and in a little while, Pooh came out from underneath it and could look around again.

"Well!" said Owl. "This is a nice state of things! What are we going to do now, Pooh?"

"Can you think of anything, Pooh?" asked Piglet.

"Because," said Owl, "we can't go out by what used to be the front door. Something has fallen on it."

"But how else *can* you go out?" asked Piglet anxiously.

"That is the problem, Piglet, to which I am asking Pooh to give his mind."

Pooh sat on the floor which had once been a wall, and gazed up at the ceiling which had once been another wall with a front door in it, and tried very hard to give his mind to it.

"Could you fly up to the letterbox with Piglet on your back?" he asked Owl.

"No," said Piglet quickly. "He couldn't."

"Because you see, Owl, if we could get Piglet into the letterbox, he might squeeze through the place where the letters come and climb down the tree and run for help."

Owl explained that he didn't have the Necessary Dorsal Muscles, and Piglet said, "Then we'd better think of something else," and he began to at once.

Pooh's mind had gone back to the day when he had saved Piglet from the flood and everybody had admired him so much. As that didn't often happen, Pooh thought he would like it to happen again. And suddenly, just as it had come to him before, an idea came to him.

"Owl," said Pooh. "I have thought of something."

"Astute and Helpful Bear," said Owl.

Pooh looked proud at being called a stout and helpful bear, and said modestly that he just happened to think of it.

He explained that if you tied a piece of string to Piglet, and flew up to the letterbox with the other end in your beak and pushed it through the wire and brought it down to the floor. Then, you and Pooh would pull hard at this end and Piglet would go slowly up at the other end. And there you were.

"There Piglet is," said Owl, "if the string doesn't break."

"And supposing it does?" asked Piglet, really wanting to know.

"It won't break," said Pooh comfortingly, "because you're a small animal and I'll stand underneath. If you save us all, it will be a Very Grand Thing to talk about afterwards."

Piglet felt much better after this. When everything was ready, he found himself slowly rising up to the ceiling. He was so proud that he would have called out "Look at me!" if he hadn't been afraid that Pooh and Owl would let go of their end of the string to look at him.

"Up we go!" said Pooh cheerfully.

"The ascent is proceeding as expected," said Owl helpfully.

Soon, it was all over. Piglet opened the letterbox, climbed in and squeezed out the other side.

Happy and excited, he turned round to squeak a last message to the prisoners.

"It's all right," he called through the letterbox. "Your tree is blown right over, Owl, and there's a branch across the door, but Christopher Robin and I will be back in about half an hour. Goodbye, Pooh!"

And without waiting to hear Pooh say, "Goodbye, and thank you, Piglet," he was off.

"Half an hour," said Owl, settling himself comfortably. "That will just give me time to finish that story I was telling you about my Uncle Robert – a portrait of whom you see underneath you. Now, where was I? Oh, yes. It was on just such a blusterous day as this that my Uncle Robert —"

Pooh closed his eyes.

This edition published in Great Britain 2002
First published in 1999 by Egmont Books Limited
239 Kensington High Street, London W8 6SA
Copyright © 2002 Michael John Brown, Peter Janson-Smith,
Roger Hugh Vaughan Charles Morgan and Timothy Michael
Robinson, Trustees of the Pooh Properties.
Published under licence from The Walt Disney Company.
Stories adapted from *The House at Pooh Corner*, first published 1928.
Text by A.A. Milne and line drawings by E.H. Shepard
copyright under the Berne Convention.
New and adapted line drawings and colouring of the illustrations
by Stuart Trotter copyright © 1996 Egmont Books Limited
All Rights Reserved.
ISBN 1 4052 0156 8
1 3 5 7 9 10 8 6 4 2
Printed in China.